THE TREE OF LIFE

THE TREE OF LIFE

by C. L. Moore

A gripping tale of the planet Mars and the terrible monstrosity that called its victims to it from afar—a tale of Northwest Smith

Over time-ruined Illar the searching planes swooped and circled. Northwest Smith, peering up at them with a steel-pale stare from the shelter of a half-collapsed temple, thought of vultures wheeling above carrion. All day long now they had been raking these ruins for him. Presently, he knew, thirst would begin to parch his throat and hunger to gnaw at him. There was neither food nor water in these ancient Martian ruins, and he knew that it could be only a matter of time before the urgencies of his own body would drive him out to signal those wheeling Patrol ships and trade his hard-won liberty for food and drink. He crouched lower under the shadow of the temple arch and cursed the accuracy of the Patrol gunner whose flame-blast had caught his dodging ship just at the edge of Illar's ruins.

Presently it occurred to him that in most Martian temples of the ancient days an ornamental well had stood in the outer court for the benefit of wayfarers. Of course all water in it would be a million years dry now, but for lack of anything better to do he rose from his seat at the edge of the collapsed central dome and made his cautious way by still intact corridors toward the front of the temple. He paused in a tangle of wreckage at the courtyard's edge and looked out across the sun-drenched expanse of pavement toward that ornate well that once had served travelers who passed by here in the days when Mars was a green planet.

It was an unusually elaborate well, and amazingly well preserved. Its rim had been inlaid with a mosaic pattern whose symbolism must once have borne deep meaning, and above it in a great fan of time-defying bronze an elaborate grille-work portrayed the inevitable tree-of-life pattern which so often appears in the symbolism of the three worlds. Smith looked at it a bit incredulously from his shelter, it was so miraculously preserved amidst all this chaos of broken stone, casting a delicate tracery of shadow on the sunny pavement as perfectly as it must have done a million years ago when dusty travelers paused here to drink. He could picture them filing in at noontime through the great gates that——

The vision vanished abruptly as his questing eyes made the circle of the ruined walls. There had been no gate. He could not find a trace of it anywhere around the outer wall of the court. The only entrance here, as nearly as he could tell from the foundations that remained, had been the door in whose ruins he now stood. Queer. This must have been a private court, then, its great grille-crowned well reserved for the use of the priests. Or wait—had there not been a priest-king Illar after whom the city was named? A wizard-king, so legend said, who ruled temple as well as palace with an iron hand. This elaborately patterned well, of material royal enough to withstand the weight of ages, might well have been sacrosanct for the use of that long-dead monarch. It might——

*

Across the sun-bright pavement swept the shadow of a plane. Smith dodged back into deeper hiding while the ship circled low over the courtyard. And it was then, as he crouched against a crumbled wall and waited, motionless, for the danger to pass, that he became aware for the first time of a sound that startled him so he could scarcely credit his ears—a recurrent sound, choked and sorrowful—the sound of a woman sobbing.

The incongruity of it made him forgetful for a moment of the peril hovering overhead in the sun-hot outdoors. The dimness of the temple ruins became a living and vital place for that moment, throbbing with the sound of tears. He looked about half in incredulity, wondering if hunger and thirst were playing tricks on him already, or if these broken halls might be haunted by a million-years-old sorrow that wept along the corridors to drive its hearers mad. There were tales of such haunters in some of Mars' older ruins. The hair prickled faintly at the back of his neck as he laid a hand on the butt of his force-gun and commenced a cautious prowl toward the source of the muffled noise.

Presently he caught a flash of white, luminous in the gloom of these ruined walls, and went forward with soundless steps, eyes narrowed in the effort to make out what manner of creature this might be that wept alone in time-forgotten ruins. It was a woman. Or it had the dim outlines of a woman, huddled against an angle of fallen walls and veiled in a fabulous shower of long dark hair. But there was something uncannily odd about her. He could not focus his pale stare upon her outlines. She was scarcely more than a luminous blot of whiteness in the gloom, shimmering with a look of unreality which the sound of her sobs denied.

*

Before he could make up his mind just what to do, something must have warned the weeping girl that she was no longer alone, for the sound of her tears checked suddenly and she lifted her head, turning to him a face no more distinguishable than her body's outlines. He made no effort to resolve the blurred features into visibility, for out of that luminous mask burned two eyes that caught his with an almost perceptible impact and gripped them in a stare from which he could not have turned if he would.

They were the most amazing eyes he had ever met, colored like moonstone, milkily translucent, so that they looked almost blind. And that magnetic stare held him motionless. In the instant that she gripped him with that fixed, moonstone look he felt oddly as if a tangible bond were taut between them.

Then she spoke, and he wondered if his mind, after all, had begun to give way in the haunted loneliness of dead Illar; for though the words she spoke fell upon his ears in a gibberish of meaningless sounds, yet in his brain a message formed with a clarity that far transcended the halting communication of words. And her milkily colored eyes bored into his with a fierce intensity.

"I'm lost—I'm lost——" wailed the voice in his brain.

A rush of sudden tears brimmed the compelling eyes, veiling their brilliance. And he was free again with that clouding of the moonstone surfaces. Her voice wailed, but the words were meaningless and no knowledge formed in his brain to match them. Stiffly he stepped back a pace and looked down at her, a feeling of helpless incredulity rising within him.

THE TREE OF LIFE

For he still could not focus directly upon the shining whiteness of her, and nothing save those moonstone eyes were clear to him.

The girl sprang to her feet and rose on tiptoe, gripping his shoulders with urgent hands. Again the blind intensity of her eyes took hold of his, with a force almost as tangible as the clutch of her hands; again that stream of intelligence poured into his brain, strongly, pleadingly.

"Please, please take me back! I'm so frightened—I can't find my way—oh, please!"

He blinked down at her, his dazed mind gradually realizing the basic facts of what was happening. Obviously her milky, unseeing eyes held a magnetic power that carried her thoughts to him without the need of a common speech. And they were the eyes of a powerful mind, the outlets from which a stream of fierce energy poured into his brain. Yet the words they conveyed were the words of a terrified and helpless girl. A strong sense of wariness was rising in him as he considered the incongruity of speech and power, both of which were beating upon him more urgently with every breath. The mind of a forceful and strong-willed woman, carrying the sobs of a frightened girl. There was no sincerity in it.

"Please, please!" cried her impatience in his brain. "Help me! Guide me back!"

"Back where?" he heard his own voice asking.

"The Tree!" wailed that queer speech in his brain, while gibberish was all his ears heard and the moonstone stare transfixed him strongly. "The Tree of Life! Oh, take me back to the shadow of the Tree!"

A vision of the grille-ornamented well leaped into his memory. It was the only tree symbol he could think of just then. But what possible connection could there be between the well and the lost girl—if she was lost? Another wail in that unknown tongue, another anguished shake of his shoulders, brought a sudden resolution into his groping mind. There could be no harm in leading her back to the well, to whose grille she must surely be referring. And strong curiosity was growing in his mind. Much more than met the eye was concealed in this queer incident. And a wild guess had flashed through his mind that perhaps she might have come from some subterranean world into which the well descended. It would explain her luminous pallor, if not her blurriness; and, too, her eyes did not seem to function in the light. There was a much more incredible explanation of her presence, but he was not to know it for a few minutes yet.

"Come along," he said, taking the clutching hands gently from his shoulders. "I'll lead you to the well."

She sighed in a deep gust of relief and dropped her compelling eyes from his, murmuring in that strange, gabbling tongue what must have been thanks. He took her by the hand and turned toward the ruined archway of the door.

Against his fingers her flesh was cool and firm. To the touch she was tangible, but even thus near, his eyes refused to focus upon the cloudy opacity of her body, the dark blur of her streaming hair. Nothing but those burning, blinded eyes were strong enough to pierce the veil that parted them.

She stumbled along at his side over the rough floor of the temple, saying nothing more, panting with eagerness to return to her incomprehensible "tree." How much of that eagerness was assumed Smith still could not be quite sure. When they reached the door he halted her for a moment, scanning the sky for danger. Apparently the ships had finished with this quarter of the city, for he could see two or three of them half a mile away, hovering low over Illar's northern section. He could risk it without much peril. He led the girl cautiously out into the sun-hot court.

*

She could not have known by sight that they neared the well, but when they were within twenty paces of it she flung up her blurred head suddenly and tugged at his hand. It was she who led him that last stretch which parted the two from the well. In the sun the shadow tracery of the grille's symbolic pattern lay vividly outlined on the ground. The girl gave a little gasp of delight. She dropped his hand and ran forward three short steps, and plunged into the very center of that shadowy pattern on the ground. And what happened then was too incredible to believe.

THE TREE OF LIFE

The pattern ran over her like a garment, curving to the curve of her body in the way all shadows do. But as she stood there striped and laced with the darkness of it, there came a queer shifting in the lines of black tracery, a subtle, inexplicable movement to one side. And with that motion she vanished. It was exactly as if that shifting had moved her out of one world into another. Stupidly Smith stared at the spot from which she had disappeared.

Then several things happened almost simultaneously. The zoom of a plane broke suddenly into the quiet, a black shadow dipped low over the rooftops, and Smith, too late, realized that he stood defenseless in full view of the searching ships. There was only one way out, and that was too fantastic to put faith in, but he had no time to hesitate. With one leap he plunged full into the midst of the shadow of the tree of life.

Its tracery flowed round him, molding its pattern to his body. And outside the boundaries everything executed a queer little sidewise dip and slipped in the most extraordinary manner, like an optical illusion, into quite another scene. There was no intervention of blankness. It was as if he looked through the bars of a grille upon a picture which without warning slipped sidewise, while between the bars appeared another scene, a curious, dim landscape, gray as if with the twilight of early evening. The air had an oddly thickened look, through which he saw the quiet trees and the flower-spangled grass of the place with a queer, unreal blending, like the landscape in a tapestry, all its outlines blurred.

In the midst of this tapestried twilight the burning whiteness of the girl he had followed blazed like a flame. She had paused a few steps away and stood waiting, apparently quite sure that he would come after. He grinned a little to himself as he realized it, knowing that curiosity must almost certainly have driven him in her wake even if the necessity for shelter had not compelled his following.

She was clearly visible now, in this thickened dimness—visible, and very lovely, and a little unreal. She shone with a burning clarity, the only vivid thing in the whole twilit world. Eyes upon that blazing whiteness, Smith stepped forward, scarcely realizing that he had moved.

Slowly he crossed the dark grass toward her. That grass was soft under-foot, and thick with small, low-blooming flowers of a shining pallor. Botticelli painted such spangled swards for the feet of his angels. Upon it the girl's bare feet gleamed whiter than the blossoms. She wore no garment but the royal mantle of her hair, sweeping about her in a cloak of shining darkness that had a queer, unreal tinge of purple in that low light. It brushed her ankles in its fabulous length. From the hood of it she watched Smith coming toward her, a smile on her pale mouth and a light blazing in the deeps of her moonstone eyes. She was not blind now, nor frightened. She stretched out her hand to him confidently.

"It is my turn now to lead you," she smiled. As before, the words were gibberish, but the penetrating stare of those strange white eyes gave them a meaning in the depths of his brain.

Automatically his hand went out to hers. He was a little dazed, and her eyes were very compelling. Her fingers twined in his and she set off over the flowery grass, pulling him beside her. He did not ask where they were going. Lost in the dreamy spell of the still, gray, enchanted place, he felt no need for words. He was beginning to see more clearly in the odd, blurring twilight that ran the outlines of things together in that queer, tapestried manner. And he puzzled in a futile, muddled way as he went on over what sort of land he had come into. Overhead was darkness, paling into twilight near the ground, so that when he looked up he was staring into bottomless deeps of starless night.

Trees and flowering shrubs and the flower-starred grass stretched emptily about them in the thick, confusing gloom of the place. He could see only a little distance through that dim air. It was as if they walked a strip of tapestried twilight in some unlighted dream. And the girl, with her lovely, luminous body and richly colored robe of hair was like a woman in a tapestry too, unreal and magical.

After a while, when he had become a little adjusted to the queerness of the whole scene, he began to notice furtive movements in the shrubs and trees they passed. Things flickered too swiftly for him to catch their outlines, but from the tail of his eye he was aware of motion, and somehow of eyes that watched. That sensation was a familiar one to him, and he kept an uneasy gaze on those shiftings in the shrubbery as they went on. Presently he caught a watcher in full view between bush and tree, and saw that it was a man, a little, furtive, dark-skinned man who dodged hastily back into cover again before Smith's eyes could do more than take in the fact of his existence.

After that he knew what to expect and could make them out more easily: little, darting people with big eyes that shone with a queer, sorrowful darkness from their small, frightened faces as they scuttled through the bushes, dodging always just out of plain sight among the leaves. He could hear the soft rustle of their passage, and once or twice when they passed near a clump of shrubbery he thought he caught the echo of little whispering calls, gentle as the rustle of leaves and somehow full of a strange warning note so clear that he caught it even amid the murmur of their speech. Warning calls, and little furtive hiders in the leaves, and a landscape of tapestried blurring carpeted with Botticelli flower-strewn sward. It was all a dream. He felt quite sure of that.

*

It was a long while before curiosity awakened in him sufficiently to make him break the stillness. But at last he asked dreamily,

"Where are we going?"

The girl seemed to understand that without the necessity of the bond her hypnotic eyes made, for she turned and caught his eyes in a white stare and answered,

"To Thag. Thag desires you."

"What is Thag?"

In answer to that she launched without preliminary upon a little singsong monolog of explanation whose stereotyped formula made him faintly uneasy with the thought that it must have been made very often to attain the status of a set speech; made to many men, perhaps, whom Thag had desired. And what became of them afterward? he wondered. But the girl was speaking.

C. L. MOORE

"Many ages ago there dwelt in Illar the great King Illar for whom the city was named. He was a magician of mighty power, but not mighty enough to fulfill all his ambitions. So by his arts he called up out of darkness the being known as Thag, and with him struck a bargain. By that bargain Thag was to give of his limitless power, serving Illar all the days of Illar's life, and in return the king was to create a land for Thag's dwelling-place and people it with slaves and furnish a priestess to tend Thag's needs. This is that land. I am that priestess, the latest of a long line of women born to serve Thag. The tree-people are his—his lesser servants.

"I have spoken softly so that the tree-people do not hear, for to them Thag is the center and focus of creation, the end and beginning of all life. But to you I have told the truth."

"But what does Thag want of me?"

"It is not for Thag's servants to question Thag."

"Then what becomes, afterward, of the men Thag desires?" he pursued.

"You must ask Thag that."

She turned her eyes away as she spoke, snapping the mental bond that had flowed between them with a suddenness that left Smith dizzy. He went on at her side more slowly, pulling back a little on the tug of her fingers. By degrees the sense of dreaminess was fading, and alarm began to stir in the deeps of his mind. After all, there was no reason why he need let this blank-eyed priestess lead him up to the very maw of her god. She had lured him into this land by what he knew now to have been a trick; might she not have worse tricks than that in store for him?

She held him, after all, by nothing stronger than the clasp of her fingers, if he could keep his eyes turned from hers. Therein lay her real power, but he could fight it if he chose. And he began to hear more clearly than ever the queer note of warning in the rustling whispers of the tree-folk who still fluttered in and out of sight among the leaves. The twilight place had taken on menace and evil.

Suddenly he made up his mind. He stopped, breaking the clasp of the girl's hand.

THE TREE OF LIFE

"I'm not going," he said.

She swung round in a sweep of richly tinted hair, words jetting from her in a gush of incoherence. But he dared not meet her eyes, and they conveyed no meaning to him. Resolutely he turned away, ignoring her voice, and set out to retrace the way they had come. She called after him once, in a high, clear voice that somehow held a note as warning as that in the rustling voices of the tree-people, but he kept on doggedly, not looking back. She laughed then, sweetly and scornfully, a laugh that echoed uneasily in his mind long after the sound of it had died upon the twilit air.

After a while he glanced back over one shoulder, half expecting to see the luminous dazzle of her body still glowing in the dim glade where he had left her; but the blurred tapestry-landscape was quite empty.

He went on in the midst of a silence so deep it hurt his ears, and in a solitude unhaunted even by the shy presences of the tree-folk. They had vanished with the fire-bright girl, and the whole twilight land was empty save for himself. He plodded on across the dark grass, crushing the upturned flower-faces under his boots and asking himself wearily if he could be mad. There seemed little other explanation for this hushed and tapestried solitude that had swallowed him up. In that thunderous quiet, in that deathly solitude, he went on.

*

When he had walked for what seemed to him much longer than it should have taken to reach his starting-point, and still no sign of an exit appeared, he began to wonder if there were any way out of the gray land of Thag. For the first time he realized that he had come through no tangible gateway. He had only stepped out of a shadow, and—now that he thought of it—there were no shadows here. The grayness swallowed everything up, leaving the landscape oddly flat, like a badly drawn picture. He looked about helplessly, quite lost now and not sure in what direction he should be facing, for there was nothing here by which to know directions. The trees and shrubs and the starry grass still stretched about him, uncertainly outlined in that changeless dusk. They seemed to go on for ever.

But he plodded ahead, unwilling to stop because of a queer tension in the air, somehow as if all the blurred trees and shrubs were waiting in breathless anticipation, centering upon his stumbling figure. But all trace of animate life had vanished with the disappearance of the priestess' white-glowing figure. Head down, paying little heed to where he was going, he went on over the flowery sward.

An odd sense of voids about him startled Smith at last out of his lethargic plodding. He lifted his head. He stood just at the edge of a line of trees, dim and indistinct in the unchanging twilight. Beyond them—he came to himself with a jerk and stared incredulously. Beyond them the grass ran down to nothingness, merging by imperceptible degrees into a streaked and arching void—not the sort of emptiness into which a material body could fall, but a solid *nothing*, curving up toward the dark zenith as the inside of a sphere curves. No physical thing could have entered there. It was too utterly void, an inviolable emptiness which no force could invade.

He stared up along the inward arch of that curving, impassable wall. Here, then, was the edge of the queer land Illar had wrested out of space itself. This arch must be the curving of solid space which had been bent awry to enclose the magical land. There was no escape this way. He could not even bring himself to approach any nearer to that streaked and arching blank. He could not have said why, but it woke in him an inner disquiet so strong that after a moment's staring he turned his eyes away.

Presently he shrugged and set off along the inside of the line of trees which parted him from the space-wall. Perhaps there might be a break somewhere. It was a forlorn hope, but the best that offered. Wearily he stumbled on over the flowery grass.

How long he had gone on along that almost imperceptibly curving line of border he could not have said, but after a timeless interval of gray solitude he gradually became aware that a tiny rustling and whispering among the leaves had been growing louder by degrees for some time. He looked up. In and out among the trees which bordered that solid wall of nothingness little, indistinguishable figures were flitting. The tree-men had returned. Queerly

15

grateful for their presence, he went on a bit more cheerfully, paying no heed to their timid dartings to and fro, for Smith was wise in the ways of wild life.

Presently, when they saw how little heed he paid them, they began to grow bolder, their whispers louder. And among those rustling voices he thought he was beginning to catch threads of familiarity. Now and again a word reached his ears that he seemed to recognize, lost amidst the gibberish of their speech. He kept his head down and his hands quiet, plodding along with a cunning stillness that began to bear results.

From the corner of his eye he could see that a little dark tree-man had darted out from cover and paused midway between bush and tree to inspect the queer, tall stranger. Nothing happened to this daring venturer, and soon another risked a pause in the open to stare at the quiet walker among the trees. In a little while a small crowd of the tree-people was moving slowly parallel with his course, staring with all the avid curiosity of wild things at Smith's plodding figure. And among them the rustling whispers grew louder.

Presently the ground dipped down into a little hollow ringed with trees. It was a bit darker here than it had been on the higher level, and as he went down the slope of its side he saw that among the underbrush which filled it were cunningly hidden huts twined together out of the living bushes. Obviously the hollow was a tiny village where the tree-folk dwelt.

He was surer of this when they began to grow bolder as he went down into the dimness of the place. The whispers shrilled a little, and the boldest among his watchers ran almost at his elbow, twittering their queer, broken speech in hushed syllables whose familiarity still bothered him with its haunting echo of words he knew. When he had reached the center of the hollow he became aware that the little folk had spread out in a ring to surround him. Wherever he looked their small, anxious faces and staring eyes confronted him. He grinned to himself and came to a halt, waiting gravely.

None of them seemed quite brave enough to constitute himself spokesman, but among several a hurried whispering broke out in which he caught the words "Thag" and "danger" and "beware." He recognized the meaning of these words without placing in his mind their origins in some tongue he knew. He knit his sun-bleached brows and concentrated harder, striving to wrest from that curious, murmuring whisper some hint of its original root. He had a smattering of more tongues than he could have counted offhand, and it was hard to place these scattered words among any one speech.

But the word "Thag" had a sound like that of the very ancient dryland tongue, which upon Mars is considered at once the oldest and the most uncouth of all the planet's languages. And with that clue to guide him he presently began to catch other syllables which were remotely like syllables from the dryland speech. They were almost unrecognizable, far, far more ancient than the very oldest versions of the tongue he had ever heard repeated, almost primitive in their crudity and simplicity. And for a moment the sheerest awe came over him, as he realized the significance of what he listened to.

*

The dryland race today is a handful of semi-brutes, degenerate from the ages of past time when they were a mighty people at the apex of an almost forgotten glory. That day is millions of years gone now, too far in the past to have record save in the vaguest folklore. Yet here was a people who spoke the rudiments of that race's tongue as it must have been spoken in the race's dim beginnings, perhaps a million years earlier even than that immemorial time of their triumph. The reeling of millenniums set Smith's mind awhirl with the effort at compassing their span.

There was another connotation in the speaking of that tongue by these timid bush-dwellers, too. It must mean that the forgotten wizard king, Illar, had peopled his sinister, twilight land with the ancestors of today's dryland dwellers. If they shared the same tongue they must share the same lineage. And humanity's remorseless adaptability had done the rest.

It had been no kinder here than in the outside world, where the ancient plains-men who had roamed Mars' green prairies had dwindled with their dying plains, degenerating at last into a shrunken, leather-skinned bestiality. For here that same race root had declined into these tiny, slinking creatures with their dusky skins and great, staring eyes and their voices that never rose above a whisper. What tragedies must lie behind that gradual degeneration!

All about him the whispers still ran. He was beginning to suspect that through countless ages of hiding and murmuring those voices must have lost the ability to speak aloud. And he wondered with a little inward chill what terror it was which had transformed a free and fearless people into these tiny wild things whispering in the underbrush.

The little anxious voices had shrilled into vehemence now, all of them chattering together in their queer, soft, rustling whispers. Looking back later upon that timeless space he had passed in the hollow, Smith remembered it as some curious nightmare—dimness and tapestried blurring, and a hush like death over the whole twilight land, and the timid voices whispering, whispering, eloquent with terror and warning.

He groped back among his memories and brought forth a phrase or two remembered from long ago, an archaic rendering of the immemorial tongue they spoke. It was the simplest version he could remember of the complex speech now used, but he knew that to them it must sound fantastically strange. Instinctively he whispered as he spoke it, feeling like an actor in a play as he mouthed the ancient idiom,

"I—I cannot understand. Speak—more slowly——"

A torrent of words greeted this rendering of their tongue. Then there was a great deal of hushing and hissing, and presently two or three between them began laboriously to recite an involved speech, one syllable at a time. Always two or more shared the task. Never in his converse with them did he address anyone directly. Ages of terror had bred all directness out of them.

"Thag," they said. "Thag, the terrible—Thag, the omnipotent—Thag, the unescapable. Beware of Thag."

For a moment Smith stood quiet, grinning down at them despite himself. There must not be too much of intelligence left among this branch of the race, either, for surely such a warning was superfluous. Yet they had mastered their agonies of timidity to give it. All virtue could not yet have been bred out of them, then. They still had kindness and a sort of desperate courage rooted deep in fear.

"What is Thag?" he managed to inquire, voicing the archaic syllables uncertainly. And they must have understood the meaning if not the phraseology, for another spate of whispered tumult burst from the clustering tribe. Then, as before, several took up the task of answering.

"Thag—Thag, the end and the beginning, the center of creation. When Thag breathes the world trembles. The earth was made for Thag's dwelling-place. All things are Thag's. Oh, beware! Beware!"

This much he pieced together out of their diffuse whisperings, catching up the fragments of words he knew and fitting them into the pattern.

"What—what is the danger?" he managed to ask.

"Thag—hungers. Thag must be fed. It is we who—feed—him, but there are times when he desires other food than us. It is then he sends his priestess forth to lure—food—in. Oh, beware of Thag!"

"You mean then, that she—the priestess—brought me in for—food?"

A chorus of grave, murmuring affirmatives.

"Then why did she leave me?"

"There is no escape from Thag. Thag is the center of creation. All things are Thag's. When he calls, you must answer. When he hungers, he will have you. Beware of Thag!"

Smith considered that for a moment in silence. In the main he felt confident that he had understood their warning correctly, and he had little reason to doubt that they knew whereof they spoke. Thag might not be the center of the universe, but if they said he could call a victim from anywhere in the land, Smith was not disposed to doubt it. The priestess' willingness to let him leave her unhindered, yes, even her scornful laughter as he looked back, told the same story. Whatever Thag might be, his power in this land could not be doubted. He made up his mind suddenly what he must do, and turned to the breathlessly waiting little folk.

"Which way—lies Thag?" he asked.

THE TREE OF LIFE

A score of dark, thin arms pointed. Smith turned his head speculatively toward the spot they indicated. In this changeless twilight all sense of direction had long since left him, but he marked the line as well as he could by the formation of the trees, then turned to the little people with a ceremonious farewell rising to his lips.

"My thanks for——" he began, to be interrupted by a chorus of whispering cries of protest. They seemed to sense his intention, and their pleadings were frantic. A panic anxiety for him glowed upon every little terrified face turned up to his, and their eyes were wide with protest and terror. Helplessly he looked down.

"I—I must go," he tried stumblingly to say. "My only chance is to take Thag unawares, before he sends for me."

He could not know if they understood. Their chattering went on undiminished, and they even went so far as to lay tiny hands on him, as if they would prevent him by force from seeking out the terror of their lives.

"No, no, no!" they wailed murmurously. "You do not know what it is you seek! You do not know Thag! Stay here! Beware of Thag!"

*

A little prickling of unease went down Smith's back as he listened. Thag must be very terrible indeed if even half this alarm had foundation. And to be quite frank with himself, he would greatly have preferred to remain here in the hidden quiet of the hollow, with its illusion of shelter, for as long as he was allowed to stay. But he was not of the stuff that yields very easily to its own terrors, and hope burned strongly in him still. So he squared his broad shoulders and turned resolutely in the direction the tree-folk had indicated.

When they saw that he meant to go, their protests sank to a wail of bitter grieving. With that sound moaning behind him he went up out of the hollow, like a man setting forth to the music of his own dirge. A few of the bravest went with him a little way, flitting through the underbrush and darting from tree to tree in a timidity so deeply ingrained that even when no immediate peril threatened they dared not go openly through the twilight.

C. L. MOORE

Their presence was comforting to Smith as he went on. A futile desire to help the little terror-ridden tribe was rising in him, a useless gratitude for their warning and their friendliness, their genuine grieving at his departure and their odd, paradoxical bravery even in the midst of hereditary terror. But he knew that he could do nothing for them, when he was not at all sure he could even save himself. Something of their panic had communicated itself to him, and he advanced with a sinking at the pit of his stomach. Fear of the unknown is so poignant a thing, feeding on its own terror, that he found his hands beginning to shake a little and his throat going dry as he went on.

*

The rustling and whispering among the bushes dwindled as his followers one by one dropped away, the bravest staying the longest, but even they failing in courage as Smith advanced steadily in that direction from which all their lives they had been taught to turn their faces. Presently he realized that he was alone once more. He went on more quickly, anxious to come face to face with this horror of the twilight and dispel at least the fearfulness of its mystery.

*

The silence was like death. Not a breeze stirred the leaves, and the only sound was his own breathing, the heavy thud of his own heart. Somehow he felt sure that he was coming nearer to his goal. The hush seemed to confirm it. He loosened the force-gun at his thigh.

In that changeless twilight the ground was sloping down once more into a broader hollow. He descended slowly, every sense alert for danger, not knowing if Thag was beast or human or elemental, visible or invisible. The trees were beginning to thin. He knew that he had almost reached his goal.

He paused at the edge of the last line of trees. A clearing spread out before him at the bottom of the hollow, quiet in the dim, translucent air. He could focus directly upon no outlines anywhere, for the tapestried blurring of the place. But when he saw what stood in the very center of the clearing he stopped dead-still, like one turned to stone, and a shock of utter cold went chilling through him. Yet he could not have said why.

21

THE TREE OF LIFE

For in the clearing's center stood the Tree of Life. He had met the symbol too often in patterns and designs not to recognize it, but here that fabulous thing was living, growing, actually springing up from a rooted firmness in the spangled grass as any tree might spring. Yet it could not be real. Its thin brown trunk, of no recognizable substance, smooth and gleaming, mounted in the traditional spiral; its twelve fantastically curving branches arched delicately outward from the central stem. It was bare of leaves. No foliage masked the serpentine brown spiral of the trunk. But at the tip of each symbolic branch flowered a blossom of bloody rose so vivid he could scarcely focus his dazzled eyes upon them.

This tree alone of all objects in the dim land was sharply distinct to the eye—terribly distinct, remorselessly clear. No words can describe the amazing menace that dwelt among its branches. Smith's flesh crept as he stared, yet he could not for all his staring make out why peril was so eloquent there. To all appearances here stood only a fabulous symbol miraculously come to life; yet danger breathed out from it so strongly that Smith felt the hair lifting on his neck as he stared.

*

It was no ordinary danger. A nameless, choking, paralyzed panic was swelling in his throat as he gazed upon the perilous beauty of the Tree. Somehow the arches and curves of its branches seemed to limn a pattern so dreadful that his heart beat faster as he gazed upon it. But he could not guess why, though somehow the answer was hovering just out of reach of his conscious mind. From that first glimpse of it his instincts shuddered like a shying stallion, yet reason still looked in vain for an answer.

*

Nor was the Tree merely a vegetable growth. It was alive, terribly, ominously alive. He could not have said how he knew that, for it stood motionless in its empty clearing, not a branch trembling, yet in its immobility more awfully vital than any animate thing. The very sight of it woke in Smith an insane urging to flight, to put worlds between himself and this inexplicably dreadful thing.

C. L. MOORE

*

Crazy impulses stirred in his brain, coming to insane birth at the calling of the Tree's peril—the desperate need to shut out the sight of that thing that was blasphemy, to put out his own sight rather than gaze longer upon the perilous grace of its branches, to slit his own throat that he might not need to dwell in the same world which housed so frightful a sight as the Tree.

*

All this was a mad battering in his brain. The strength of him was enough to isolate it in a far corner of his consciousness, where it seethed and shrieked half heeded while he turned the cool control which the spaceways life had taught him to the solution of this urgent question. But even so his hand was moist and shaking on his gun-butt, and the breath rasped in his dry throat.

Why—he asked himself in a determined groping after steadiness—should the mere sight of a tree, even so fabulous a one as this, rouse that insane panic in the gazer? What peril could dwell invisibly in a tree so frightful that the living horror of it could drive a man mad with the very fact of its unseen presence? He clenched his teeth hard and stared resolutely at that terrible beauty in the clearing, fighting down the sick panic that rose in his throat as his eyes forced themselves to dwell upon the Tree.

Gradually the revulsion subsided. After a nightmare of striving he mustered the strength to force it down far enough to allow reason's entry once more. Sternly holding down that frantic terror under the surface of consciousness, he stared resolutely at the Tree. And he knew that this was Thag.

It could be nothing else, for surely two such dreadful things could not dwell in one land. It must be Thag, and he could understand now the immemorial terror in which the tree-folk held it, but he did not yet grasp in what way it threatened them physically. The inexplicable dreadfulness of it was a menace to the mind's very existence, but surely a rooted tree, however terrible to look at, could wield little actual danger.

As he reasoned, his eyes were seeking restlessly among the branches, searching for the answer to their dreadfulness. After all, this thing wore the

23

THE TREE OF LIFE

aspect of an old pattern, and in that pattern there was nothing dreadful. The tree of life had made up the design upon that well-top in Illar through whose shadow he had entered here, and nothing in that bronze grille-work had roused terror. Then why——? What living menace dwelt invisibly among these branches to twist them into curves of horror?

A fragment of old verse drifted through his mind as he stared in perplexity: What immortal hand or eye could frame thy fearful symmetry?

And for the first time the true significance of a "fearful symmetry" broke upon him. Truly a more than human agency must have arched these subtle curves so delicately into dreadfulness, into such an awful beauty that the very sight of it made those atavistic terrors he was so sternly holding down leap in a gibbering terror.

A tremor rippled over the Tree. Smith froze rigid, staring with startled eyes. No breath of wind had stirred through the clearing, but the Tree was moving with a slow, serpentine grace, writhing its branches leisurely in a horrible travesty of voluptuous enjoyment. And upon their tips the blood-red flowers were spreading like cobra's hoods, swelling and stretching their petals out and glowing with a hue so eye-piercingly vivid that it transcended the bounds of color and blazed forth like pure light.

But it was not toward Smith that they stirred. They were arching out from the central trunk toward the far side of the clearing. After a moment Smith tore his eyes away from the indescribably dreadful flexibility of those branches and looked to see the cause of their writhing.

A blaze of luminous white had appeared among the trees across the clearing. The priestess had returned. He watched her pacing slowly toward the Tree, walking with a precise and delicate grace as liquidly lovely as the motion of the Tree. Her fabulous hair swung down about her in a swaying robe that rippled at every step away from the moon-white beauty of her body. Straight toward the Tree she paced, and all the blossoms glowed more vividly at her nearness, the branches stretching toward her, rippling with eagerness.

Priestess though she was, he could not believe that she was going to come within touch of that Tree the very sight of which roused such a panic instinct

24

of revulsion in every fiber of him. But she did not swerve or slow in her advance. Walking delicately over the flowery grass, arrogantly luminous in the twilight, so that her body was the center and focus of any landscape she walked in, she neared her horribly eager god.

Now she was under the Tree, and its trunk had writhed down over her and she was lifting her arms like a girl to her lover. With a gliding slowness the flame-tipped branches slid round her. In that incredible embrace she stood immobile for a long moment, the Tree arching down with all its curling limbs, the girl straining upward, her head thrown back and the mantle of her hair swinging free of her body as she lifted her face to the quivering blossoms. The branches gathered her closer in their embrace. Now the blossoms arched near, curving down all about her, touching her very gently, twisting their blazing faces toward the focus of her moon-white body. One poised directly above her face, trembled, brushed her mouth lightly. And the Tree's tremor ran unbroken through the body of the girl it clasped.

*

The incredible dreadfulness of that embrace was suddenly more than Smith could bear. All his terrors, crushed down with so stern a self-control, without warning burst all bounds and rushed over him in a flood of blind revulsion. A whimper choked up in his throat and quite involuntarily he swung round and plunged into the shielding trees, hands to his eyes in a futile effort to blot out the sight of lovely horror behind him whose vividness was burnt upon his very brain.

Heedlessly he blundered through the trees, no thought in his terror-blank mind save the necessity to run, run, run until he could run no more. He had given up all attempt at reason and rationality; he no longer cared why the beauty of the Tree was so dreadful. He only knew that until all space lay between him and its symmetry he must run and run and run.

What brought that frenzied madness to an end he never knew. When sanity returned to him he was lying face down on the flower-spangled sward in a silence so deep that his ears ached with its heaviness. The grass was cool against his cheek. For a moment he fought the back-flow of knowledge into his emptied mind. When it came, the memory of that horror he had fled from, he started up with a wild thing's swiftness and glared around pale-eyed into the unchanging dusk. He was alone. Not even a rustle in the leaves spoke of the tree-folk's presence.

For a moment he stood there alert, wondering what had roused him, wondering what would come next. He was not left long in doubt. The answer was shrilling very, very faintly through that aching quiet, an infinitesimally tiny, unthinkably far-away murmur which yet pierced his ear-drums with the sharpness of tiny needles. Breathless, he strained in listening. Swiftly the sound grew louder. It deepened upon the silence, sharpened and shrilled until the thin blade of it was vibrating in the center of his innermost brain.

And still it grew, swelling louder and louder through the twilight world in cadences that were rounding into a queer sort of music and taking on such an unbearable sweetness that Smith pressed his hands over his ears in a futile attempt to shut the sound away. He could not. It rang in steadily deepening intensities through every fiber of his being, piercing him with thousands of tiny music-blades that quivered in his very soul with intolerable beauty. And he thought he sensed in the piercing strength of it a vibration of queer, unnamable power far mightier than anything ever generated by man, the dim echo of some cosmic dynamo's hum.

*

The sound grew sweeter as it strengthened, with a queer, inexplicable sweetness unlike any music he had ever heard before, rounder and fuller and more complete than any melody made up of separate notes. Stronger and stronger he felt the certainty that it was the song of some mighty power, humming and throbbing and deepening through the twilight until the whole dim land was one trembling reservoir of sound that filled his entire consciousness with its throbbing, driving out all other thoughts and realizations, until he was no more than a shell that vibrated in answer to the calling.

For it was a calling. No one could listen to that intolerable sweetness without knowing the necessity to seek its source. Remotely in the back of his mind Smith remembered the tree-folk's warning, "When Thag calls, you must answer." Not consciously did he recall it, for all his consciousness was answering the siren humming in the air, and, scarcely realizing that he moved, he had turned toward the source of that calling, stumbling blindly over the flowery sward with no thought in his music-brimmed mind but the need to answer that lovely, power-vibrant summoning.

Past him as he went on moved other shapes, little and dark-skinned and ecstatic, gripped like himself in the hypnotic melody. The tree-folk had forgotten even their inbred fear at Thag's calling, and walked boldly through the open twilight, lost in the wonder of the song.

Smith went on with the rest, deaf and blind to the land around him, alive to one thing only, that summons from the siren tune. Unrealizingly, he retraced the course of his frenzied flight, past the trees and bushes he had blundered through, down the slope that led to the Tree's hollow, through the thinning of the underbrush to the very edge of the last line of foliage which marked the valley's rim.

*

By now the calling was so unbearably intense, so intolerably sweet that somehow in its very strength it set free a part of his dazed mind as it passed the limits of audible things and soared into ecstasies which no senses bound. And though it gripped him ever closer in its magic, a sane part of his brain was waking into realization. For the first time alarm came back into his mind, and by slow degrees the world returned about him. He stared stupidly at the grass moving by under his pacing feet. He lifted a dragging head and saw that the trees no longer rose about him, that a twilit clearing stretched away on all sides toward the forest rim which circled it, that the music was singing from some source so near that—that—

The Tree! Terror leaped within him like a wild thing. The Tree, quivering with unbearable clarity in the thick, dim air, writhed above him, blossoms blazing with bloody radiance and every branch vibrant and undulant to the tune of that unholy song. Then he was aware of the lovely, luminous

27

THE TREE OF LIFE

whiteness of the priestess swaying forward under the swaying limbs, her hair rippling back from the loveliness of her as she moved.

Choked and frenzied with unreasoning terror, he mustered every effort that was in him to turn, to run again like a mad-man out of that dreadful hollow, to hide himself under the weight of all space from the menace of the Tree. And all the while he fought, all the while panic drummed like mad in his brain, his relentless body plodded on straight toward the hideous loveliness of that siren singer towering above him. From the first he had felt subconsciously that it was Thag who called, and now, in the very center of that ocean of vibrant power, he knew. Gripped in the music's magic, he went on.

All over the clearing other hypnotized victims were advancing slowly, with mechanical steps and wide, frantic eyes as the tree-folk came helplessly to their god's calling. He watched a group of little, dusky sacrifices pace step by step nearer to the Tree's vibrant branches. The priestess came forward to meet them with outstretched arms. He saw her take the foremost gently by the hands. Unbelieving, hypnotized with horrified incredulity, he watched her lead the rigid little creature forward under the fabulous Tree whose limbs yearned downward like hungry snakes, the great flowers glowing with avid color.

He saw the branches twist out and lengthen toward the sacrifice, quivering with eagerness. Then with a tiger's leap they darted, and the victim was swept out of the priestess' guiding hands up into the branches that darted round like tangled snakes in a clot that hid him for an instant from view. Smith heard a high, shuddering wail ripple out from that knot of struggling branches, a dreadful cry that held such an infinity of purest horror and understanding that he could not but believe that Thag's victims in the moment of their doom must learn the secret of his horror. After that one frightful cry came silence. In an instant the limbs fell apart again from emptiness. The little savage had melted like smoke among their writhing, too quickly to have been devoured, more as if he had been snatched into another dimension in the instant the hungry limbs hid him. Flame-tipped, avid, they were dipping now toward another victim as the priestess paced serenely forward.

*

And still Smith's rebellious feet were carrying him on, nearer and nearer the writhing peril that towered over his head. The music shrilled like pain. Now he was so close that he could see the hungry flower-mouths in terrible detail as they faced round toward him. The limbs quivered and poised like cobras, reached out with a snakish lengthening, down inexorably toward his shuddering helplessness. The priestess was turning her calm white face toward his.

*

Those arcs and changing curves of the branches as they neared were sketching lines of pure horror whose meaning he still could not understand, save that they deepened in dreadfulness as he neared. For the last time that urgent wonder burned up in his mind why—*why* so simple a thing as this fabulous Tree should be infused with an indwelling terror strong enough to send his innermost soul frantic with revulsion. For the last time—because in that trembling instant as he waited for their touch, as the music brimmed up with unbearable, brain-wrenching intensity, in that one last moment before the flower-mouths seized him—he saw. He understood.

*

With eyes opened at last by the instant's ultimate horror, he saw the real Thag. Dimly he knew that until now the thing had been so frightful that his eyes had refused to register its existence, his brain to acknowledge the possibility of such dreadfulness. It had literally been too terrible to see, though his instinct knew the presence of infinite horror. But now, in the grip of that mad, hypnotic song, in the instant before unbearable terror enfolded him, his eyes opened to full sight, and he saw.

That Tree was only Thag's outline, sketched three-dimensionally upon the twilight. Its dreadfully curving branches had been no more than Thag's barest contours, yet even they had made his very soul sick with intuitive revulsion. But now, seeing the true horror, his mind was too numb to do more than register its presence: Thag, hovering monstrously between earth and heaven, billowing and surging up there in the translucent twilight, tethered to the ground by the Tree's bending stem and reaching ravenously after the hypnotized fodder that his calling brought helpless into his clutches. One by one he snatched them up, one by one absorbed them into the great, unseeable horror of his being. That, then, was the reason why they vanished so instantaneously, sucked into the concealing folds of a thing too dreadful for normal eyes to see.

The priestess was pacing forward. Above her the branches arched and leaned. Caught in a timeless paralysis of horror, Smith stared upward into the enormous bulk of Thag while the music hummed intolerably in his shrinking brain—Thag, the monstrous thing from darkness, called up by Illar in those long-forgotten times when Mars was a green planet. Foolishly his brain wandered among the ramifications of what had happened so long ago that time itself had forgotten, refusing to recognize the fate that was upon himself. He knew a tingle of respect for the ages-dead wizard who had dared command a being like this to his services—this vast, blind, hovering thing, ravenous for human flesh, indistinguishable even now save in those terrible outlines that sent panic leaping through him with every motion of the Tree's fearful symmetry.

*

All this flashed through his dazed mind in the one blinding instant of understanding. Then the priestess' luminous whiteness swam up before his hypnotized stare. Her hands were upon him, gently guiding his mechanical footsteps, very gently leading him forward into—into——

*

The writhing branches struck downward, straight for his face. And in one flashing leap the moment's infinite horror galvanized him out of his paralysis. Why, he could not have said. It is not given to many men to know the ultimate essentials of all horror, concentrated into one fundamental unit. To most men it would have had that same paralyzing effect up to the very instant of destruction. But in Smith there must have been a bed-rock of subtle violence, an unyielding, inflexible vehemence upon which the structure of his whole life was reared. Few men have it. And when that ultimate intensity of terror struck the basic flint of him, reaching down through mind and soul into the deepest depths of his being, it struck a spark from that inflexible barbarian buried at the roots of him which had force enough to shock him out of his stupor.

*

In the instant of release his hand swept like an unloosed spring, of its own volition, straight for the butt of his power-gun. He was dragging it free as the Tree's branches snatched him from its priestess' hands. The fire-colored blossoms burnt his flesh as they closed round him, the hot branches gripping like the touch of ravenous fingers. The whole Tree was hot and throbbing with a dreadful travesty of fleshly life as it whipped him aloft into the hovering bulk of incarnate horror above.

In the instantaneous upward leap of the flower-tipped limbs Smith fought like a demon to free his gun-hand from the gripping coils. For the first time Thag knew rebellion in his very clutches, and the ecstasy of that music which had dinned in Smith's ears so strongly that by now it seemed almost silence was swooping down a long arc into wrath, and the branches tightened with hot insistency, lifting the rebellious offering into Thag's monstrous, indescribable bulk.

But even as they rose, Smith was twisting in their clutch to maneuver his hand into a position from which he could blast that undulant tree trunk into nothingness. He knew intuitively the futility of firing up into Thag's imponderable mass. Thag was not of the world he knew; the flame blast might well be harmless to that mighty hoverer in the twilight. But at the Tree's root, where Thag's essential being merged from the imponderable to the material, rooting in earthly soil, he should be vulnerable if he were vulnerable at all. Struggling in the tight, hot coils, breathing the nameless essence of horror, Smith fought to free his hand.

The music that had rung so long in his ears was changing as the branches lifted him higher, losing its melody and merging by swift degrees into a hum of vast and vibrant power that deepened in intensity as the limbs drew him upward into Thag's monstrous bulk, the singing force of a thing mightier than any dynamo ever built. Blinded and dazed by the force thundering through every atom of his body, he twisted his hand in one last, convulsive effort, and fired.

He saw the flame leap in a dazzling gush straight for the trunk below. It struck. He heard the sizzle of annihilated matter. He saw the trunk quiver convulsively from the very roots, and the whole fabulous Tree shook once with an ominous tremor. But before that tremor could shiver up the branches to him the hum of the living dynamo which was closing round his body shrilled up arcs of pure intensity into a thundering silence.

Then without a moment's warning the world exploded. So instantaneously did all this happen that the gun-blast's roar had not yet echoed into silence before a mightier sound than the brain could bear exploded outward from the very center of his own being. Before the awful power of it everything reeled into a shaken oblivion. He felt himself falling....

*

A queer, penetrating light shining upon his closed eyes roused Smith by degrees into wakefulness again. He lifted heavy lids and stared upward into the unwinking eye of Mars' racing nearer moon. He lay there blinking dazedly for a while before enough of memory returned to rouse him. Then he sat up painfully, for every fiber of him ached, and stared round on a scene of the wildest destruction. He lay in the midst of a wide, rough circle which held nothing but powdered stone. About it, rising raggedly in the moving moonlight, the blocks of time-forgotten Illar loomed.

But they were no longer piled one upon another in a rough travesty of the city they once had shaped. Some force mightier than any of man's explosives seemed to have hurled them with such violence from their beds that their very atoms had been disrupted by the force of it, crumbling them into dust. And in the very center of the havoc lay Smith, unhurt.

He stared in bewilderment about the moonlight ruins. In the silence it seemed to him that the very air still quivered in shocked vibrations. And as he stared he realized that no force save one could have wrought such destruction upon the ancient stones. Nor was there any explosive known to man which would have wrought this strange, pulverizing havoc upon the blocks of Illar. That force had hummed unbearably through the living dynamo of Thag, a force so powerful that space itself had bent to enclose it. Suddenly he realized what must have happened.

Not Illar, but Thag himself had warped the walls of space to enfold the twilit world, and nothing but Thag's living power could have held it so bent to segregate the little, terror-ridden land inviolate.

Then when the Tree's roots parted, Thag's anchorage in the material world failed and in one great gust of unthinkable energy the warped space-walls had ceased to bend. Those arches of solid space had snapped back into their original pattern, hurling the land and all its dwellers into—into——His mind balked in the effort to picture what must have happened, into what ultimate dimension those denizens must have vanished.

Only himself, enfolded deep in Thag's very essence, the intolerable power of the explosion had not touched. So when the warped space-curve ceased to be, and Thag's hold upon reality failed, he must have been dropped back out of the dissolving folds upon the spot where the Tree had stood in the space-circled world, through that vanished world-floor into the spot he had been snatched from in the instant of the dim land's dissolution. It must have happened after the terrible force of the explosion had spent itself, before Thag dared move even himself through the walls of changing energy into his own far land again.

Smith sighed and lifted a hand to his throbbing head, rising slowly to his feet. What time had elapsed he could not guess, but he must assume that the Patrol still searched for him. Wearily he set out across the circle of havoc toward the nearest shelter which Illar offered. The dust rose in ghostly, moonlit clouds under his feet.